ROSE AND DOROTHY

WRITTEN AND ILLUSTRATED BY
ROSLYN SCHWARTZ

ORCHARD BOOKS
New York

Copyright © 1990 by Roslyn Schwartz
First American Edition 1991 published by Orchard
Books. First published in Canada by Kids Can Press, Ltd.

Orchard Books
A division of Franklin Watts, Inc.
387 Park Avenue South, New York, NY 10016

Manufactured in the United States of America.
Printed by General Offset Company, Inc. Bound by
Horowitz/Rae. Book design by Jean Krulis.

10 9 8 7 6 5 4 3 2 1

The text of this book is set in 20 pt. Zapf
International Medium.

Library of Congress Cataloging-in-Publication Data
Schwartz, Roslyn. Rose and Dorothy / written and
illustrated by Roslyn Schwartz. — 1st American ed.
p.   cm.   Summary: A mouse and an elephant learn to
live together in peace. ISBN 0-531-05918-9.
ISBN 0-531-08518-X (lib. bdg.) [1. Mice—Fiction.
2. Elephants—Fiction.   3. Friendship—Fiction.]
I. Title. PZ7.S41128Ro   1991   [E]—dc20   90-43013

Rose lived all by herself in a house with too many rooms.

Then she met Dorothy and invited her to move in.

To Rose, Dorothy was larger than life and twice as charming.

They went shopping together.

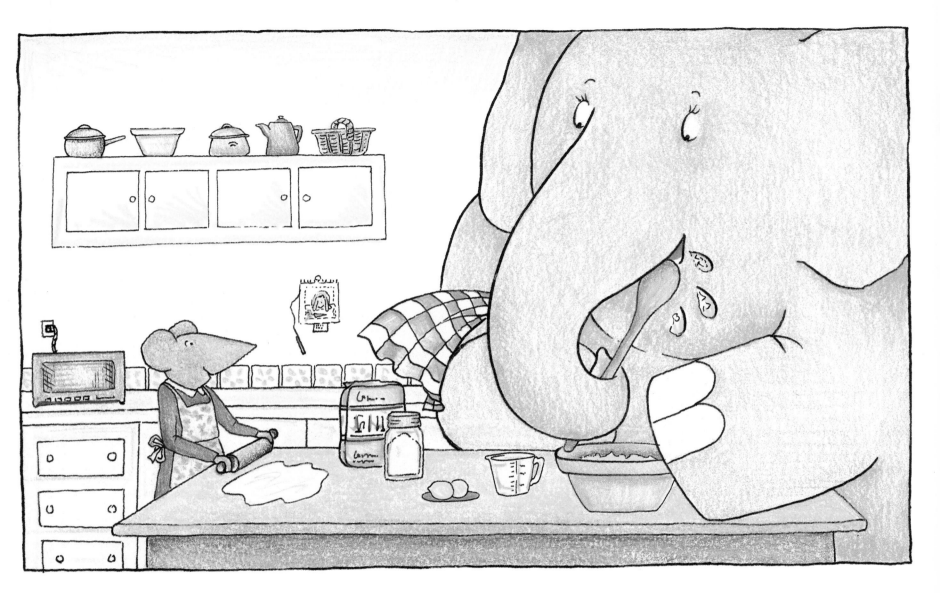

And cooked together.

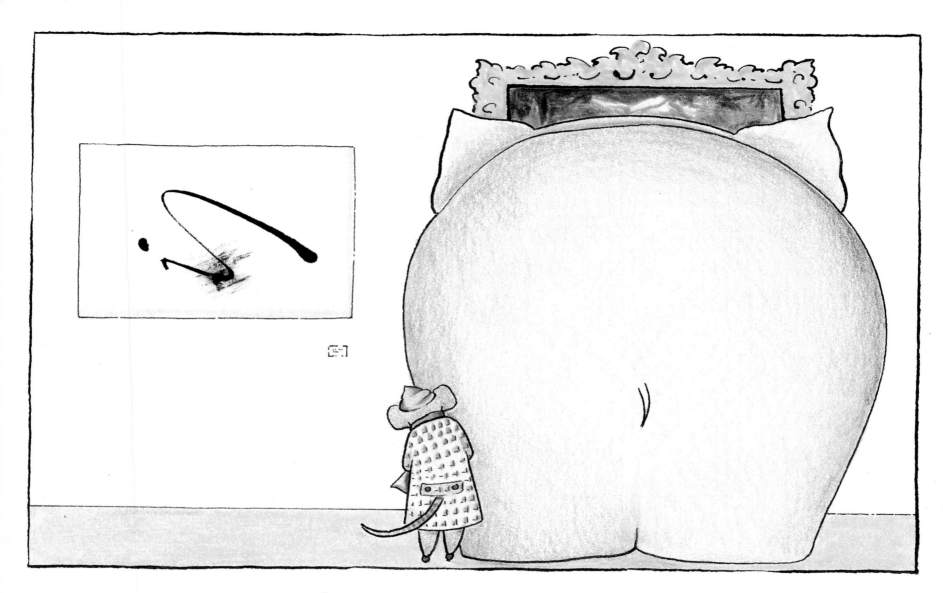

They went to the art gallery.

And entertained often.

Dorothy loved to sing.

They even went on vacation together.
(Dorothy seemed to tan faster than Rose.)

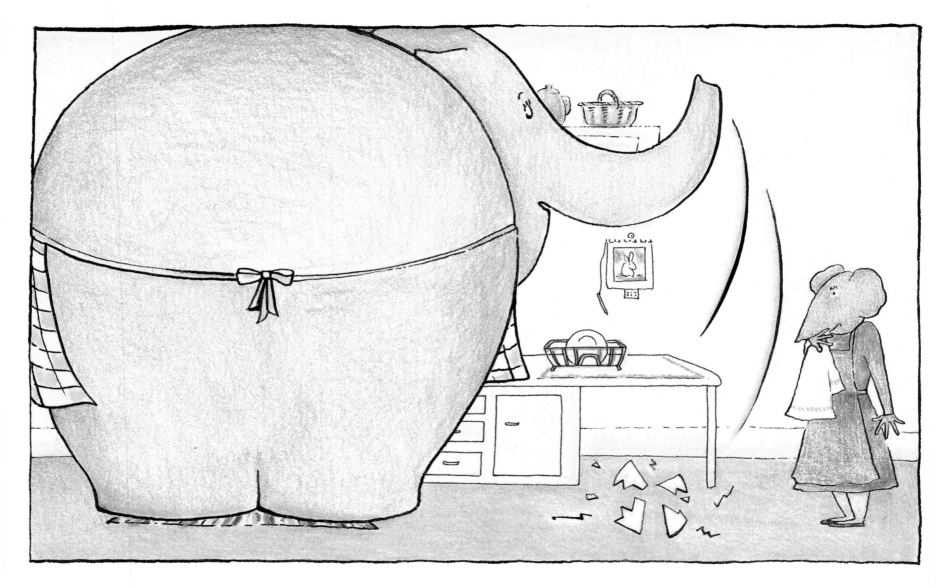

Then one day, Rose thought, "How clumsy she is."

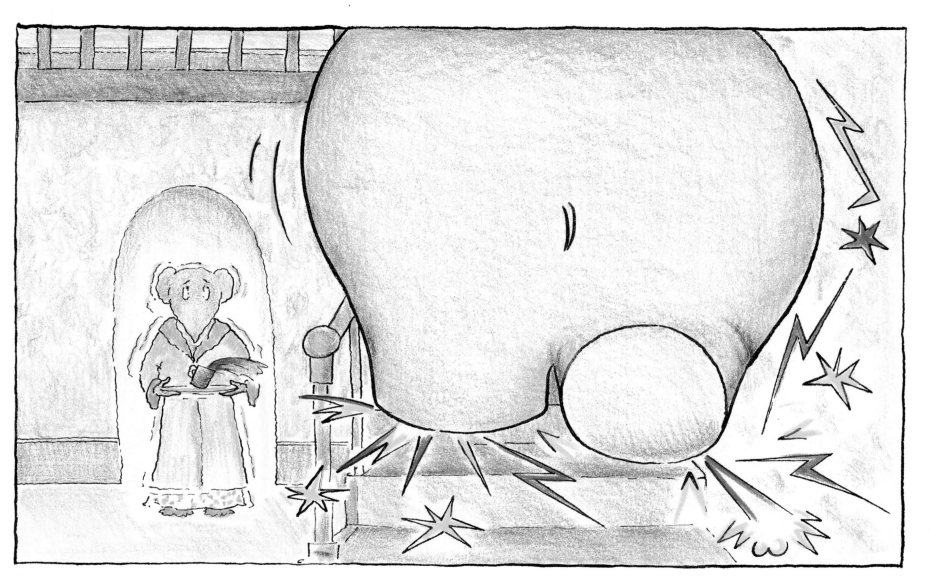

"And how noisy!"

"And how messy!"

Rose hid in her room.

Then in her bed.

Finally, she fled next door.

Her neighbor, Alice, was very kind.

She poured tea from a pot with two spouts and served cookies.

Rose talked and talked. Alice listened.

Dorothy listened, too.

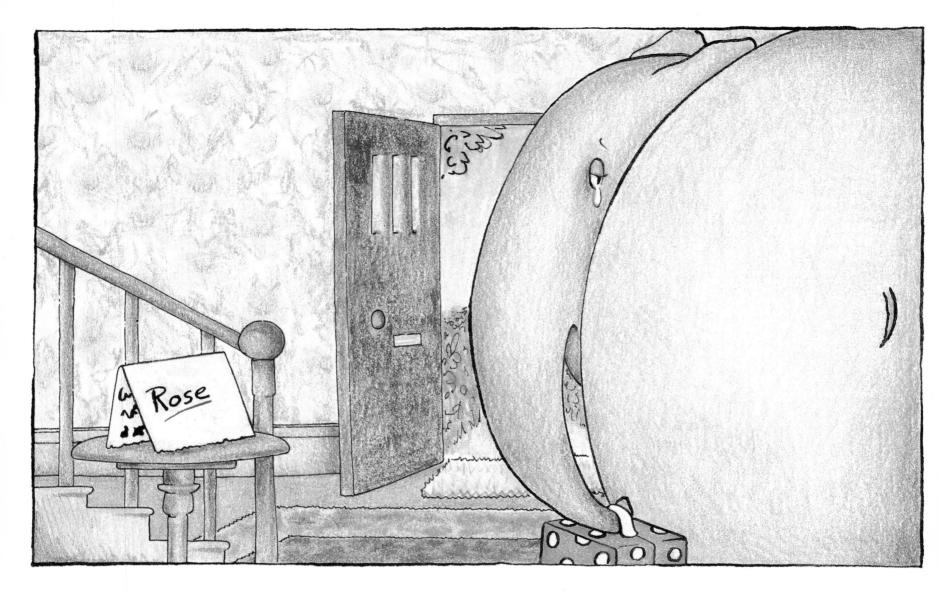

Dorothy packed her bag and left Rose a note.

Lost in the city, tired, and hungry, she could go no further.

"Oooowooooh!" she sobbed.
"What will I do? I can't live in the park forever."

"I'll get a job."

Dorothy was an overnight success.

Rose was heartbroken and alone.

She called Dorothy. They talked and talked.

Dorothy bought the big house next to Rose and Alice.

They all saw one another often,
and Rose and Dorothy were friends for life.